P9-CRD-900

PROPHECY OF EVIL

MYSTICONS

PROPHECY OF EVIL

SADIE CHESTERFIELD

[Imprint]
MAKE YOUR MARK

NEW YORK

[Imprint]
MAKE YOUR MARK

A part of Macmillan Publishing Group, LLC
175 Fifth Avenue, New York, NY 10010

Mʏsticons: Prophecy of Evil. Mysticons characters, designs, and elements
© 2018 Nelvana Limited. Mysticons is a trademark of Nelvana Limited.
All rights reserved. Printed in the United States of America by
LSC Communications, Harrisonburg, Virginia.

Library of Congress Cataloging-in-Publication Data is available.

ISBN 978-125-0-16512-1 (paperback) / ISBN 978-1-250-16511-4 (ebook)

Our books may be purchased in bulk for promotional, educational, or business
use. Please contact your local bookseller or the Macmillan Corporate and
Premium Sales Department at (800) 221-7945 ext. 5442 or by e-mail at
MacmillanSpecialMarkets@macmillan.com.

Book design by Heather Palisi

Imprint logo designed by Amanda Spielman

First edition, 2018

1 3 5 7 9 10 8 6 4 2

mackids.com

If you should make this book your own
without paying its fair cost
into a pen of angry griffins
you will soon find yourself tossed!

ONE

THE MYSTICONS STOOD next to the Celestial Forge, a great ancient furnace in the Astromancer Academy. The bubbling metal at its core lit the room with a fiery glow, and the noise of its bellows sounded like an angry wind.

The Mysticons were four girls gifted with incredible, ancient powers. And right now, they were wondering if their latest plan was really going to work.

They stared up at the Dragon Disk they'd made just days before, after the real one had been stolen from them. It floated in the air, the same size and shape as the original artifact, but a dull gray color. They looked to it to tell them the prophecy they'd heard so much about. But would their duplicate Disk work?

Nova Terron, leader of the Astromancers, stood frowning in the corner. The decision to copy the Dragon Disk had been made without him, and he was clearly doubtful about it. Arkayna, leader of the Mysticons, didn't want to think about how he'd act if their plan was a failure.

High above, the full moon shone through the skylight in the great, cavernous room. As the amber glow hit the Disk, it projected runes in mid-air. The Mysticons' plan had succeeded! They stared at the message, transfixed.

When twin stars unite, the spectral beast will take flight.
Its roars will herald a new dark age, and the realm will be purged by the dragon's rage.

Choko, the little foz who followed the Mysticons everywhere—even to places not always friendly to small furry animals—was so terrified he dove behind Piper, his tail shaking in fear.

"Spectral beast? A new dark age?" Em said, panic in her voice.

"You're the expert," Zarya said to Nova Terron. "What's it all mean?" The Astromancers were an ancient order of mages dedicated to helping the Mysticons in their fight against evil, so Zarya figured if anyone could decode the message, it was the leader of the Astromancers.

Nova Terron felt very worried about what it meant. "Doom, Mysticon Ranger . . ." he told her. His deep voice sounded even deeper than normal as he repeated, "Doom."

He could barely look at them. His face was tense with worry. "Gandobi, assemble the Astromancers," he said into his phone.

"But, Star Master," Gandobi, one of the

Astromancers, said from the other end, "it's Card Night—"

"It may be your last if you do not meet us at the Caves of the Fang immediately!" Nova shot back. Then he turned on his heel, heading deeper into the Academy.

Arkayna followed him out the door, determined to find out more, and the other Mysticons trailed behind her. She was the princess of Gemina and the daughter of Queen Goodfey. For as long as she could remember, her mother had taught her to defend the Dragon Disk, an ancient artifact that was kept in the castle treasury. Just weeks before, the Disk had started glowing again, and soon bestowed powers on a new group of Mysticons. Arkayna had been transformed into the fierce, fireball-shooting Mysticon Dragon Mage. Like the other Mysticons, when Arkayna was in her guise as the Dragon Mage, few knew her true identity as Princess Arkayna. Even the

Astromancers knew her only as the Mysticon Dragon Mage.

Emerald "Em" Goldenbraid had been Arkayna's griffin wrangler at the castle. Em had become the Mysticon Knight, with an energy shield and a powerful sword. They were joined by two street kids, a savvy human orphan named Zarya Moonwolf and a naïve elf named Piper Willowbrook. Zarya had been transformed into the Mysticon Ranger, with a bow and magic arrows, and Piper had become the Mysticon Striker, with hoops made of pure energy—perfect for tossing at bad guys.

Together the new Mysticons had unified all four pieces of the Codex—an ancient book of Mysticon magic—and found the Dragon Disk, but both had been stolen and used to summon a queen of evil, Necrafa. She was now using her minion Tazma to try to destroy the entire realm.

Key to that plan was stealing a hidden

prophecy from the Astromancers, which Tazma and Necrafa had pulled off just a few days before. But now the Mysticons had the prophecy. They had all the same clues Necrafa did, and Arkayna was just beginning to realize what they meant.

"So we're hunting a dragon?" Arkayna asked.

"Thousands of years ago, a spectral drake rose from the caves and wreaked havoc and destruction," Nova Terron explained. "It nearly destroyed Gemina. If there is a new dragon about to rise—"

"That's where we'll find it," Malvaron added. "The Caves of the Fang."

"But the prophecy says the twin stars have to unite," Arkayna said.

"Focus on the quest at hand, Dragon Mage," Nova Terron snapped. "Necrafa and Tazma are no doubt trying to find the Spectral Dragon even as we speak."

Arkayna fell back, stung. Why was Nova Terron being so short with her? Why wouldn't he explain the rest of the prophecy? Since when was it a bad idea to decipher every line, or to think too much about a riddle's meaning?

She lagged behind the rest of the group, repeating the prophecy in her head. There was definitely more to it than Nova Terron was telling her. . . .

TWO

ARKAYNA SWOOPED DOWN, landing her griffin out-side the Caves of the Fang. Nova Terron had brought Gandobi, Proxima, and many of the other Astromancers along with them. Gandobi had been an Astromancer for a long time, but Proxima was among the youngest in the order.

As the group assembled outside the gaping entrance to the caves, Proxima muttered, "It's about time. Tazma's already inside."

"Step aside, please, heroes coming through." Arkayna waved at her fellow Mysticons to follow her. She'd always been annoyed by Proxima, who acted like a know-it-all. "Looks like a classic dungeon crawl. Come on, girls, we've got this."

"I'll tell you what you've got," Proxima snapped. "You've gotten us into a heap of trouble."

"Says the armchair Astromancer," Zarya shot back.

"Yeah, you should try being on the front lines sometime," Arkayna said, glaring at Proxima. It was easy to have opinions when you weren't the one dodging Tazma's swirling dark magic. Maybe Arkayna had made some mistakes, but every day she was fighting back. Every day she was trying.

"Come along, Proxima," Nova Terron said as he walked out in front.

Arkayna couldn't believe her ears. "What? She's coming with us?"

"As am I," Nova Terron said. "The Spectral Dragon is a near-unstoppable force of evil. You will need all the help you can get."

"What about me?" Malvaron asked.

"What about you?" Nova Terron said. "Proxima did an in-depth study of the caves."

"You're on guard duty with us," Gandobi said, yanking Malvaron back by the ear.

"Let's go, girls," Proxima said, pushing Arkayna aside as she entered the mouth to the caves. "It's magic hour."

"Hey! That's my line," Arkayna shrieked. "My line!"

Proxima started walking into the darkness, calling behind her, "These caves run for miles under Drake City, and their center is the cavern that spawns these monsters."

Arkayna hated that they were following Proxima, listening to her give directions. It was enough to drive any mage crazy.

They turned right, then left, winding through the maze of tunnels. Until suddenly, Proxima stopped in place. She stared at the dead end ahead, then pulled out her parchment map.

"It doesn't make sense," she said. "This tunnel

should come to a branch. Maybe there's a clue in the prophecy. . . . How does it go?"

"When twin stars unite," Zarya recited.

"The spectral beast will take flight," Piper added.

Proxima furrowed her brows. "When twin stars unite? Does that mean the twin stars of Samara?"

"That's what I thought," Arkayna said, "but their orbits don't cross for another . . ."

Em closed her eyes, doing the math in her head. "Twelve years, four hours, and six minutes."

"Please stop this jabber about stars!" Nova Terron grumbled. "We need to focus on finding the dragon."

When Zarya looked at him, he wouldn't meet her gaze. "That's what we're doing. Hey, you know something, don't you? What are you hiding?"

"Nothing! Nothing! See, this is my hiding-nothing face." Nova Terron whistled a quick tune and smiled.

"The prophecy's not talking about stars, is it?" Arkayna asked.

For a moment everyone was silent. "No," Nova Terron finally admitted. "It speaks of the royal twins."

"But there haven't been any twins born to the royal family," Arkayna said, studying his expression. Why was Nova Terron acting so weird? What was he even talking about? Royal twins?

"So, we don't have to worry about the dragon, right?" Piper said hopefully.

"Wrong," Nova Terron replied. "There *are* twins. They were born fifteen years ago. To Queen Goodfey."

Arkayna could only stare at him. *My mother had twins?* she thought.

THREE

ARKAYNA FELT LIKE she was falling through the sky. She was breathless, terrified, looking for something—anything—to hold on to. If what Nova Terron said was true, she . . . no, *they* . . .

Arkayna remembered that she was disguised as the Mysticon Dragon Mage. She had to word her question carefully. "Princess Arkayna has a twin sister?" she asked. She could barely get the words out.

"I've said too much," Nova Terron added. "We must focus on finding the dragon." He turned around and started back out of the tunnel, but Zarya blocked his path.

"Where is she?" Arkayna demanded.

"Hers is a tragic story," Nova Terron said. "She was taken at birth."

"What?" Arkayna said, feeling a lump rise in the back of her throat. Em put a hand on Arkayna's shoulder to steady her, but she couldn't help herself: "Whoever did this needs to be brought to justice! Who took her?"

But again, Nova Terron was silent. He seemed scared, uncertain. They waited for him to explain, but he didn't.

"*You* took the twin?" Em finally asked.

"Yes, I took her," he admitted. "But you have to understand—"

Arkayna lost control. Before he could say another word, she unleashed a fireball at Nova Terron, sending him tumbling across the ground. Arkayna brought her staff up over her shoulder.

She could feel her friends behind her, trying to pull her away, but she resisted.

"Get away from him!" Proxima yelled.

"How could you?" Arkayna demanded. Fire surged through her body as her friends dragged her back, away from Nova Terron. "How could you?"

Another blast of powerful magic charged through her veins, sending her flying toward Nova Terron. The other Mysticons were thrown backward.

There was a strange hum, then a beeping sound. Arkayna looked across the tunnel at a line of runes in the sand. Her friends had hit a booby trap. Any second, the runes would explode.

"Take cover!" Zarya yelled.

Within seconds, the tunnel rumbled. There was an explosion of light and heat, and rocks rained down from the cave ceiling. Arkayna could barely see anything through the dust and smoke. She heard Zarya shout for them to follow her, but Arkayna couldn't figure out where.

As she ran forward, dodging rocks and debris, she spotted Nova Terron in front of her. He ran a few feet before some rocks fell onto him.

"Go on! Go without me!" he yelled, waving Arkayna off.

She glanced up, seeing it all in slow motion. A boulder above him—now shaken free from the cave's roof—was already falling. She reached her hand out, blasting it with another fireball. It exploded into hundreds of pieces.

"You and I aren't done!" she called out.

She could feel the tunnel coming apart. Every inch of it was shaking, its roof about to fall in. She dove toward Nova Terron, bringing him with her to the other end of the tunnel. They rolled to safety just as a huge section of the ceiling caved in. Dozens of boulders fell, separating them from the others.

When the dust finally settled, Arkayna just sat there, trying to catch her breath.

"Dragon Mage?" Nova Terron asked in a small voice as he rubbed his eyes. "Dragon Mage, are you okay?"

"I'm fine, Star Master," Arkayna said, levitating him with her magic. "You're the one who should be worried."

Arkayna pushed him back into the cave wall. He stayed there, staring at her in disbelief.

"You put the quest in jeopardy so you could threaten me?" he said, an edge to his voice.

"So I could get answers!" Arkayna yelled as she sent a torrent of rocks flying toward him. "What did you do with the twin?"

"The twins had to be separated," Nova Terron said. "In order to protect the realm. To protect millions of innocent lives."

"Where did you take her?" Arkayna asked.

"Alpha Galaga, my Star Master, left specific instructions. I was to open a portal to the astral plane and"—he paused, as if it was hard for him to even say it—"may Gygax have mercy on me . . . What have I done?"

He fell to his knees, tears welling in his eyes. He hid his face in his hands, but Arkayna could tell he was crying. She'd never seen him so broken, but she still couldn't bring herself to feel sorry for him. He'd stolen an infant—her twin sister—away from her mother just because someone had told him to. Just because he was following some stupid order.

"You're worse than the monsters we fight," she said. "When this quest is over, so are you and I."

FOUR

ARKAYNA STARTED DOWN a dark tunnel. Fire still surged through her hands. With each step she grew angrier with Nova Terron. What did he mean, "to protect the realm"? How could a newborn baby do anything wrong? Hadn't her sister deserved a chance to grow up with Arkayna, to have a real family? To be loved?

She turned down another tunnel. She could hear him following along behind her, but she didn't bother to turn around. She kept going, and as they got closer to the dragon's lair, the tunnel became littered with broken weapons. There were skeletons and piles of dusty treasure. She picked up a sword and it turned to dust.

"Fallen dragon hunters and thieves from a bygone era," Nova Terron said.

Arkayna pointed at the glowing green light at the end of the tunnel. "The dragon's lair . . ." she said, starting toward it. "I'm going in."

"I'm coming with you," Nova Terron said. "We must fight as one if we wish to survive."

Arkayna just stared at him. "I'll fight 'as one' to save the realm. But for your survival? Not a chance."

She started back down the tunnel, getting closer to the lair. There was a small ledge above the opening and she walked up to it to survey the scene. Dozens of green crystals floated near the ceiling, like little islands. An egg was perched on the center one, held up by shards of green rock.

"It appears we're not hunting a dragon," Nova Terron said, "but rather its egg."

"The twins need to be united for the egg to spawn the dragon," Arkayna realized.

"Yes," Nova Terron said, arching an eyebrow. "but if we destroy the egg—"

Arkayna had a vision of the baby dragon that could hatch from that egg, and she was angry all over again. "Maybe that's how you operate," Arkayna snapped. "But not me. We take the egg and keep it safe from Necrafa."

"No, it must be destroyed," Nova Terron argued. "It is the only way to prevent—"

An evil laugh split the air. Arkayna and Nova Terron looked up to see Tazma and General Tibion, the leader of Necrafa's spectres. When Necrafa returned to life, she transformed Tibion and his army of skeleton warriors into spectres— horrible winged monsters. With Tazma and Tibion perched on one of the crystal formations high above, the army of spectres couldn't be far behind. "You can't stop fate," Tazma called out. "The end of days is inevitable!"

Tazma shot a bolt of dark magic at Arkayna and Nova Terron, knocking them off their feet. Then Tazma flew up to retrieve the egg. Arkayna blasted her with a green fireball from her Dragon Staff, then tossed another bolt around Tazma's ankle, throwing her off-course. As soon as she had a chance, she grabbed Nova Terron and rocketed him along with her to a crystal island high above.

But Tibion was closing in on the egg. Nova Terron hit him with a blast of his full power, giving Arkayna an opening. She flew to the egg. It was so close . . . she could almost reach it. . . .

Before she could grab it, Tibion shot his own blast of dark magic, sending her hurtling over the side of the crystal. Arkayna tried to climb back up, using all her might, but the rock was too slick.

Nova Terron leapt up to get the egg, but Tazma shot dark shadow tendrils at him, tying him up. She raised him into the air in front of her and smiled. "Your time has come, 'Star

Master.' And you, Dragon Mage," she said, turning to Arkayna, "you're a fool to think you can stop the Queen of the Undead."

Tazma grabbed the dragon's egg from its crystal perch. "Tibion, finish them," she snarled.

Tibion's hand glowed crimson red. He hovered in the air in front of Nova Terron, bringing his magic down just inches from Nova's face. Just as Tibion was about to end him, a pixie blast hit him from the side.

Arkayna glanced up to see her friends (well, her friends and Proxima) perched on a ledge high above. Zarya expertly shot arrows at Nova Terron, freeing him from the black tendrils that tied him up without so much as nicking him.

"Awww, what a cute dragon egg," Piper said, glaring at Tazma.

"It won't be so cute once it spawns," Tibion spat.

"Not gonna happen," Em snapped.

Arkayna climbed back up onto the crystal

ledge. "You're outnumbered. There's nothing you can do."

The Mysticons aimed their weapons at Tazma, ready to fight.

"Think again, Mysticons," Tazma said.

Before Arkayna could do anything, Tazma blasted dark magic into the roof of the cave, shattering a hole in it. The explosion rocked the crystal islands, sending shards raining down on the girls. Em threw up her shield to protect Zarya, Piper, and Proxima, but Arkayna was left exposed. A rock hit her and she flew off the island, plummeting toward the ground, far below.

"Hang on, I gotcha!" Zarya fired a cable arrow straight down, the cord catching around Arkayna's ankle. Em and Piper rushed in behind her, grabbing the end of the cord and yanking with all their might. When they finally pulled it taut, Arkayna was hanging in midair, her head mere inches from the floor. She looked up just in time to see Tibion and Tazma escape through the hole in the cave's roof, the dragon's egg clutched tightly in Tazma's hands.

Nova Terron didn't waste any time. He shot out of the roof, following Tazma and Tibion, with Mysticons and Proxima in his telekinetic grip. As soon as they were in the sky he released everyone right above their griffins. One by one, the Mysticons fell onto the giant creatures, with Nova Terron taking a seat behind Arkayna. Proxima joined Em on her griffin.

Tazma was still in their sights.

"Stop the Shadow Mage at all costs!" Nova Terron yelled.

But Tibion and his army of spectres had already closed ranks around Tazma to protect her. They descended in a barrage of dark magic, trying to knock the Mysticons off their griffins.

"Out of my way!" Arkayna cried, holding up her bracer. Her Dragon avatar emerged from her bracer and spread its giant green wings, blasting through a row of spectres. Em, Piper, and Zarya all followed, letting their avatars explode into the sky. The Wolf, the Battle Unicorn, and the Phoenix all charged toward Tibion, while Arkayna remained focused on the fleeing Tazma.

"The Dragon Mage will never stop her," Tibion laughed. Then he turned to his army of spectres, ordering them to fight. "Finish them, finish them all!"

FIVE

ARKAYNA TOOK OFF in front, Nova Terron sitting behind her on her griffin, Izzie. They flew after Tazma, chasing her out across the city. Arkayna shot fireballs at her, and Nova Terron blasted her with magic missiles, but they always seemed to just miss her. She shot back dark, swirling black tendrils, which they ducked and swerved to avoid.

"Excellent, Dragon Mage," Nova Terron said. "We're closing the distance."

Tazma must've realized the same thing, because she was staring up at a crane far above them. Hanging down from it was a bundle of metal beams held together by a chain. Before Arkayna could figure out what she was doing, Tazma blasted the chain apart, sending the beams raining down on them.

"Hang on!" Arkayna yelled. She dipped and swerved, trying to dodge all of the metal beams. As hard as she tried, there were just too many. Within seconds one knocked Nova Terron off Izzie. He went spiraling toward the street below.

"So long, Dragon Mage!" Tazma laughed an evil laugh.

Arkayna watched as Tazma zoomed away. She had no choice. She swooped down, racing toward Nova Terron. She blasted the metal beam away from him with a fireball. Then she pulled him back onto Izzie. They landed in an alley below.

He opened his eyes and looked around. "Tazma? Where is she?"

"She escaped," Arkayna said.

"You should have left me!" Nova Terron cried.

"Believe me, I wanted to." It was the truth. Arkayna could feel the tears coming back, stinging her eyes. "How could you do what you did?"

"Because it had to be done," Nova Terron said. "Why are you taking this so personally?"

"Because this is as personal as it gets," Arkayna shot back. "She was my sister."

Arkayna turned toward him and dispelled her Mysticon Dragon Mage mask. Finally, Nova Terron could see her true identity. She was Princess Arkayna, the other twin. The one who was left behind.

"Why did you do it?" she asked again, the tears coming fast. "Why?"

"I'm sorry, Your Highness," Nova Terron said softly. "Alpha Galaga ordered me to."

Nova Terron went on, telling Arkayna about the night he went to retrieve her sister. He'd gone into Drake City Tower and cast a spell on her mother, so she would only remember one child, not two. He was supposed to take the baby to

Alpha Galaga, but he couldn't bring himself to do it. Instead he brought her to a kind lady named Mrs. Sparklebottom. The last time he saw the child, she was being carried away by light pixies. *Do not fear, little one,* he'd said. *You'll be safe here.*

"I put the whole realm in jeopardy," Nova Terron said sadly.

Arkayna hugged him, her sadness lifting. Her sister was alive. He had saved her, even though he wasn't supposed to. "No—you did the right thing," she said.

"Dragon Mage!" a familiar voice called out.

Green magic flew around Arkayna as she resumed her disguise as the Mysticon Dragon Mage. Moments later, Em swooped down on her griffin with Proxima beside her, and Piper and Zarya following close behind. "Are you okay?" Em asked.

Piper put her arm around Nova Terron, trying to comfort him. "There, there, big Nova," she said, "don't cry."

"The twin is alive," Arkayna told the others. As soon as she said it, she felt her spirit rise. "We have to find her."

"Don't worry, girl," Zarya said. "We will."

"Wherever she might be," Em agreed.

Arkayna wiped the tears from her eyes. Now that Tazma and Necrafa had the dragon's egg, there was so little time. She had to find her sister. The whole realm depended on it.

SIX

"PLEASE," NOVA TERRON said, glancing around the Star Chamber. "I would urge calm."

"Calm!" Gandobi cried. "You separated the twins! And you kept this knowledge from the council. From *me*?"

"When Tazma probed your mind to learn the secret of the prophecy—" Proxima started.

"She no doubt uncovered *this* secret," Gandobi said. "Of the princess and her twin!"

"That is why we need to find the twin before Necrafa does," Arkayna said. They had been discussing the twins all morning. The rest of the

Astromancers felt betrayed that Nova Terron hadn't told them what had happened all those years before.

"How in the heavens do we do that? No one knows anything about her!" Gandobi said.

"One person does," Nova Terron corrected him. "Hortensia Q. Sparklebottom."

Piper's high-pitched giggle split the air. "Sparklebottom?"

Nova Terron ignored her. "She is the matron of the orphanage I sent the girl to. She keeps records of each child she takes in."

"Find the file, find the twin!" Em said hopefully.

"Yes, but no one cares for children as fiercely as Mrs. Sparklebottom," Nova Terron said. Again Piper laughed, and again Nova Terron ignored her. "She will protect that information with her life."

"And I'd risk my life to get it," Arkayna said.

"Just tell us where to find this"—Zarya paused, glancing sideways at Piper—"Mrs. *S*."

"The location of her sanctuary is cloaked by fairy magic," Nova Terron explained. "This spell will guide you there." He lit up Arkayna's Dragon Staff with magical energy. "The fate of the realm lies in your hands, Dragon Mage."

The Mysticons were just about to leave when Proxima stepped in front of them. "Hold on just a parsec," she said. "What about the princess?"

"Necrafa could come for her!" Gandobi cried.

Arkayna froze. She tried to keep her expression calm. No one besides the Mysticons and Nova Terron knew her real identity. It was safer that way.

"The princess can take care of herself," Arkayna said. "Trust me."

"With all due respect, why should we trust you?" Proxima insisted. "There's only one sure way to prevent the prophecy—by keeping the princess under lock and key."

Arkayna was about to argue with her, but the other Astromancers murmured their agreement. She looked to Nova Terron, hoping he'd say something in her defense, but he didn't. "Very well," he finally agreed. "By order of the council, Princess Arkayna will be kept under guard in these hallowed halls . . . indefinitely."

Arkayna smiled, trying not to let her panic show. How could she find her twin if she was trapped inside the Astromancer Academy?

While the rest of the Mysticons prepared for their mission, Arkayna followed Nova Terron into the hallway. As soon as they were out of sight of the rest of the Astromancers, she pleaded with him. "The others can't find the orphanage without me!"

Choko, who'd been listening to the whole conversation, jumped onto Arkayna's shoulder. He seemed as annoyed at Nova Terron as she was. He let out an angry chirp.

"But you can't accompany them and be here as well," Nova Terron said. "Unless . . ."

They both looked at Choko.

"I can be in two places at once," Arkayna said, realizing what Nova Terron meant. She tossed some foz snacks onto the ground, distracting Choko. He chewed happily on the Jackalope Jerky as Nova Terron moved in on him, casting a spell. "By the power of the skies, let this creature be disguised. . . ."

In an instant, Choko was transformed into a spitting image of Princess Arkayna. He had two big strips of Jackalope Jerky coming out of his mouth, and he didn't speak English, but it was still very convincing.

"Oh my goblin!" Arkayna smiled. "He—*she's* perfect."

Princess Arkayna was perched on the ground

like an animal. She lifted her foot up and used it to scratch behind her ear.

"*Almost* perfect," Arkayna corrected.

"Come along, Princess," Nova Terron said, helping Choko to his back feet. "I must protect you."

SEVEN

DAY HAD BROKEN as Arkayna led the Mysticons through the dense forest, casting aside fallen trees and branches. She kept her eyes on the end of her Dragon Staff, letting Nova Terron's spell lead the way.

"Faster, girls!" she yelled. "Give it all you've got!"

They were getting close, so close. Arkayna stopped in front of a giant bush, double-checking they were in the right place. "We're here," she said. "Mrs. Sparklebottom's sanctuary."

"So how do we get in?" Zarya asked.

Arkayna stared at the scene in front of her. It didn't look like anything special. It was just a giant tree trunk with a lotus flower in front of it. But then the lotus flower opened, revealing a tiny pixie sitting behind a tiny desk.

"Lateensia?" Arkayna said, recognizing the pixie answering the phone. It was her stepbrother Gawayne's on-again-off-again girlfriend. "You work here?"

"I'm a volunteer," Lateensia sighed.

"We need to speak to Mrs. Sparklebottom," Arkayna said.

"Yeah, I'd like to, but no," Lateensia said flatly.

"We're the Mysticons and we're on an important quest," Em tried.

"Sorry, not sorry!" Lateensia said in a sing-sing voice. "But the only things allowed inside are pixies and drooling little germ bags."

The Mysticons stared at the tree trunk. All of a sudden the door slid back, revealing a swirling blue portal. A siren blared. A big fuzzy baby with several eyes sucked on a pacifier as it floated out. Before the baby could get even a foot beyond the door, tiny pixies swarmed it and brought it back inside. Arkayna looked to the other Mysticons, wondering if they were thinking what she was thinking.

"Fine," she said. "We'll leave, right . . . now!"

But instead of leaving they all ran straight for the portal, trying to get inside before it closed.

But Lateensia was too fast. She hit a button and the portal shut. All four Mysticons slammed into it.

"Mrs. Sparklebottom's Sanctuary, a safe haven for special children," Lateensia said, answering the phone.

Arkayna, Em, Piper, and Zarya picked themselves up and stomped off into the woods, ignoring a smiling Lateensia.

"She makes me so mad!" Piper growled. She scrunched her nose and did her best Lateensia impression: *"Only pixies and babies get in. . . ."*

"That's it!" Arkayna said, getting an idea. She pulled up a recipe on her bracer. "Okay, I need youthroot, beetlebark, and primrose petals, stat!"

Piper disappeared into the woods, coming back a few minutes later with a handful of different ingredients. Arkayna telekinetically hovered them in front of her face, then combined them with magic. In an instant, she'd turned them into two separate vials of purple liquid.

"Drink this," she said, handing one to Zarya. "It's not dangerous."

"That's your pitch?" Zarya said, furrowing her brows.

"It's the only way we're going to find my sister," Arkayna said. "Please, Z?"

"The things I do for you," Zarya said, rolling her eyes. She gulped down the liquid in one shot. Then . . . *Poof!* She shrunk down to a tiny, toddler-size version of herself, complete with pigtails and a magic orb rattle.

"WHAT DID YOU DO?!" she shrieked, looking down at her new body.

"Only pixies and babies are allowed in," Arkayna explained.

"So turn me into a pixie, genius!" Zarya yelled.

"Huh . . . I guess that was an option." Arkayna smiled. But wasn't this much more fun? At least for everyone but Zarya?

"Un-baby me!" Zarya demanded.

"You can un-baby yourself," Arkayna said, giving her the second vial of liquid—the antidote. "*After* you get in. Now, cry."

She yanked the orb rattle out of Zarya's hand and set her down in front of the bush, rushing behind it to hide. Zarya's lower lip trembled and suddenly she burst into tears, her wails echoing through the forest.

It didn't take long for a flock of pixies to emerge from the orphanage. They swaddled baby Zarya in a blanket and floated her through the portal, the wood door sliding shut behind them.

EIGHT

ARKAYNA STOOD BEHIND the bush with Em and Piper, waiting and watching. They kept thinking it would only be a few minutes before Zarya opened the portal for them. But a few minutes passed, and a few more, and there was still no sign of her.

"What's taking her so long?" Arkayna asked.

"Don't worry," Piper said. "Zarya always comes through. She'll open the portal."

"Sure, but how do we get past her?" Em asked, pointing at Lateensia.

They all stared at the tiny doorkeeper. There was no way she was going to let them simply walk right into the orphanage.

"We just need a little distraction. . . ." Arkayna said. She dialed a number on her bangle-phone, then watched as Lateensia's phone rang. Arkayna pinched her nose and did her best Gawayne impersonation. "It's, like, totally Gawayne."

"Oh my goblinnnn," Lateensia cooed. "You've called me, like, five times today already."

"Ew, he did?!?" Arkayna asked, forgetting herself for a moment. Then she went right back to Gawayne's voice: "I mean—ew, I did! But I totally had to call again."

"Why?" Lateensia asked.

"Because I . . . I wanted to hear about your day?" Arkayna asked, not sure if that was the right answer.

"Gawaaaaayne!" Lateensia whined. "You never ask me that! That's totes adorbs! So, like, first I saw a flower or whatever and that was supes amazing. . . ."

She went on and on, eventually talking about some crazy dream she'd had. Arkayna stood there, her eyes on the portal, waiting. She could barely listen to Lateensia's babble.

"Oh man, I can smell my brain burning," Em muttered. "Hurry up, Zarya. Please."

But ten more minutes passed. What was Zarya doing in there? Had she gotten caught? All she had to do was go inside and—

Just when Arkayna thought she couldn't stand hearing another word, the portal swirled open. Lateensia had spun around in her chair while she talked on the phone, so her back was to the tree.

"Go! Go! Go!" Arkayna said, urging Em and Piper out of the woods.

The girls ran as fast as they could toward the portal, diving through just before it closed. Before

Arkayna could even stand up, Zarya hurled a pacifier at her head. "You," she snapped. "Fix this."

The girls all sat there, staring at her. She was still two feet tall, a little baby version of herself.

"The potion didn't work?" Em asked.

"I wouldn't know," Zarya grumbled. "This floating freak broke it."

The same baby who'd tried to escape earlier was now floating right in front of them. It was furry and pink, with four green eyes that stared back at them. It was sucking on a pacifier.

"Awwww, he's adorable!" Piper cried. "I'm going to call you . . . Blinky!"

"Focus, people! And . . . weird eyeball thingy," Arkayna said, poking the furry pink creature with her finger. "We need to find that file."

"I'm guessing it's up there." Em pointed to the top of the tree. There was a small, circular window with a balcony just outside it up top. That had to be where Mrs. Sparklebottom was.

"Let's go, girls," Arkayna said as she leapt from branch to branch. "It's magic hour."

The rest of the Mysticons followed—or tried to. Zarya's arms and legs were too tiny for her to get anywhere without Em helping her. It took them twice as long to get up to Mrs. Sparklebottom's.

The girls stood in the window, staring at the back of Mrs. Sparklebottom's head. She was watching television, but by the sound of it she'd fallen asleep. Her snores echoed through the room.

Piper crept in first, tiptoeing so she didn't make a sound.

"Fan out and look for a safe," Arkayna whispered.

Within just a few feet, Zarya tripped and fell. She was about to cry when Piper shoved a pacifier into her mouth. "Walking's hard, huh, Baby Z?"

"It's not me, it's the floor," Zarya snapped back quietly. "It's uneven."

"Look!" Piper said in hushed tones, pointing to designs that went around the room. "Pretty symbols."

"Those are the star signs of Gemina," Em said under her breath, leaning down to examine them.

Arkayna crept out from her hiding place behind a desk and stared at the symbols. They were arranged in a circle across the floor—and there was a keyhole underneath each one. "The safe is part of the floor," she breathed.

"Thirteen signs, thirteen keys," Zarya whispered. "We just need to figure out the right key to use under the right symbol." She pointed to a gold key ring sitting next to Mrs. Sparklebottom. By now the old woman had woken up and was singing along to some jingles on the TV. She was so transfixed by the screen, she still hadn't noticed they were there.

Zarya walked over to the keys as quietly as she

could, but before she could grab them, they were picked up by a telekinetic beam. The Mysticons turned to see the furry pink baby floating in the window. It had followed them there!

It lifted the keys up, over Mrs. Sparklebottom's head, and then dropped them. Arkayna leapt lightly forward and caught them before they came clattering down. She and Zarya hovered behind the couch, terrified. They didn't move until they were certain Mrs. Sparklebottom hadn't heard them.

Arkayna crawled across the floor, studying the symbols. "I was born on the tenth day of the month of the Dragon," she murmured, finding the symbol that matched her birth month. "At the stroke of midnight."

She flipped through the gold keys on the key ring, searching for the one that matched the dragon symbol. She tried it in the keyhole underneath the symbol, and it worked. Suddenly a short column of jewels rose out of part of the floor. They were arranged by different birth times.

"Ten o'clock," Arkayna mumbled, moving down a row of gems, "eleven . . . midnight!"

Zarya pointed to a green gem on the column. "There! That's your twin's birth gem."

Arkayna grabbed at it, but it fell and clinked across the floor. Thankfully Mrs. Sparklebottom had chosen that exact moment to stir her tea, and her spoon made the same clinking sound. The girls let out a deep breath and took off, turning the key to set the column back in the floor.

They leapt off the balcony and flew from branch to branch, not stopping until they were back in the nursery. Arkayna hit the button beside the door.

"Quick, everyone out!" she called.

"I'm way ahead of you," Zarya said, racing toward the swirling light. But as soon as she crossed the threshold an alarm blared: *BABY BREACH! BABY BREACH!* The girls looked down at Zarya's leg. She had a black bracelet around her ankle, and now it was flashing red.

"It's a security bracelet!" Zarya yelled. "Run!"

NINE

BEFORE THE MYSTICONS could escape from the orphanage, a giant, sticky web snagged them all. They were suspended from the tree branches above, tangled up in their own individual cocoons. They looked up at the balcony, finally seeing Mrs. Sparklebottom . . . all of her. She had eight spiderlike legs, and she was glaring down at them over her tiny black glasses.

"Nobody takes my babies!" she roared. She shot another sticky web from her hand and snatched Zarya from the group so she could hold her in her arms.

"Give her back! She's not yours!" Piper yelled. She twisted and turned, trying to free herself, but it was no use.

"Just like this birth gem you stole isn't mine?" Mrs. Sparklebottom asked, grabbing the green gem from Arkayna's hand. "I never give up information about my babies. Nor do I look kindly on those who steal it."

She raised one of her long, sharp spider legs, about to strike the final blow on the three Mysticons she'd trapped.

"She's Princess Arkayna's twin!" Arkayna blurted out.

Mrs. Sparklebottom cut Arkayna's cocoon open in one swift motion, letting her drop toward the floor. "What did you say?" She hopped down from her perch on the balcony.

"And she's in terrible danger," Arkayna went on. "If we don't find her—"

"I will!" a familiar voice interrupted. There was an explosion of black smoke at the portal into the nursery. Tazma appeared in the doorway with her shadow henchmen. She shot a blast of magic at Mrs. Sparklebottom, sending her flying. The green gem skidded across the floor.

"You'll never get the gem!" Arkayna said, about to dive for it.

But Tazma was too fast. She blasted the tree branches across the nursery. Arkayna gasped as she realized that hidden among the branches were sleeping babies, safely cocooned in webs from Mrs. Sparklebottom. But Tazma's blasts were breaking those branches, sending babies into freefall. Thinking fast, Arkayna broke the Mysticons' cocoons with magic from her Dragon Staff. "Protect the babies!" she yelled.

The girls leapt across the nursery. Piper caught two babies in her hands, and Em caught another two in her shield. As Arkayna rushed to save the others with telekinesis, Tazma stole the gem. She let out an evil laugh.

"Finish them!" she said, ordering her shadow

henchmen forward. They crept toward the Mysticons, their beady red eyes narrowing. Just before they could strike, Mrs. Sparklebottom flew up into the air, landing between the Mysticons and the shadows.

"NO ONE HURTS MY BABIES!" Mrs. Sparklebottom yelled.

She swiped at the shadows with her long, sharp legs, destroying them one by one. She ran toward another baby they'd surrounded, grabbing it before they could move in. Then she tossed a shadow at Tazma, knocking her to the ground. Tazma lost hold of the gem and it bounced across the floor again.

Zarya rushed in and grabbed it, while singing, "Nah na na nah nah!" at Tazma.

Tazma shot dark tendrils at Zarya, tying her up. She raised the baby Mysticon into the air and smiled. "Children should be neither seen nor heard. . . ." With that, she tossed Zarya over the side of the railing.

The Mysticons stood there, helpless. They all had their arms full with babies. Just when they were certain Zarya was gone, she floated up in a giant pink bubble. The furry pink baby had saved her using its telekinetic powers.

"Good boy, Blinky!" Zarya cheered. "Good boy!"

But it wasn't long before the shadows returned. The Mysticons were completely surrounded. How could they protect the babies and fight Tazma's shadow henchmen? It seemed impossible.

Suddenly Blinky's eyes began to glow. With a sudden, powerful pink blast, he disintegrated all of the shadows around them.

"That baby is terrifying!" Em said, smiling with relief.

"Can we adopt him?" Piper asked.

Arkayna wanted to laugh, but she couldn't. "Where's Tazma?" she asked.

They stared at the open portal. Tazma had escaped . . . and she had the gem.

TEN

ARKAYNA FLEW AFTER Tazma, pursuing her through the woods.

"You can attack me," Tazma said, flying above her. "But if anything happens to this, you'll never find her."

"True," Arkayna said, weighing her options. "But at least she'd be safe from you. Unleash the Dragon!"

Her Dragon avatar emerged from her bracer and knocked Tazma off course. Howling, she dropped the gem on the ground and it shattered, all of its beautiful green magic gone.

Arkayna watched as a furious Tazma flew away.

What am I supposed to do with this? she wondered as she stared at the gray pieces of glass. She fought back tears. *There's no way I'll find my sister now. . . .*

But there *was* another way. When Arkayna got back to the orphanage, Mrs. Sparklebottom said, "You know, the birth gems aren't the only place I keep information. I remember every single baby who passes through my portal." She tapped her forehead and magically pulled out a thread of memory. It turned into an image of her memory of the baby.

The baby floated up in front of Arkayna, who gasped. She would recognize that face anywhere. . . .

By the time Arkayna returned to the Astromancer Academy, she could barely contain herself. She finally had the answer she'd needed for so long. She rushed into the Star Chamber, now dressed as the princess. Choko had already transformed back. Before she could tell Nova Terron what happened, Proxima blasted through the wall.

"Reveal yourself!" Proxima said, pointing at Arkayna. "Who are you?"

Arkayna's stomach dropped. Nova Terron's spell must not have made Choko as convincing a princess as they had hoped. Proxima obviously knew something was up. She pulled at Arkayna's cheeks and hair, trying to see if it was a mask.

"Hey, hands off the princess!" Em said, pushing her back.

"She's not the princess!" Proxima yelled.

"I can assure you, I am definitely the princess," Arkayna said calmly. She felt Choko trembling against her leg, terrified Proxima might look at him.

As soon as she spoke, Proxima seemed to settle down. Arkayna was sure Choko had messed up their plan. He'd probably chirped too many times or crawled into a corner and peed on something.

"The princess has important news," Nova Terron said.

"The Mysticons found the identity of my twin," Arkayna said, turning to Proxima. She stared into her green eyes, trying to see herself in them. Wondering if Proxima already knew, if she'd felt it somehow.

"Well, who is it?" Proxima said, searching Arkayna's face.

"It's you," Arkayna said. "We're sisters."

They stood there, staring at each other. Arkayna couldn't believe it was true. Would she ever feel close to Proxima? Had that been why Proxima annoyed her so much? Was it some normal, sisterly thing she hadn't understood?

She took a deep breath, trying to steady herself. She hoped one day this would all make sense. . . .

ELEVEN

PIPER RAN ACROSS the Stronghold common room with Choko in her hands. He was curled up into a ball, so every few feet she bounced him off the floor. She dodged Em, spun around, and dunked Choko into a portal bag that hung on the wall. There was another portal bag right next to it, and he traveled between them, popping out of the other one.

"Slam-dunka-bunga!" she cheered.

Piper and Em had been playing portal bag with Choko all morning. He'd gone from one to the other again and again. Arkayna sat there, trying to enjoy herself, but it was no use. Since they'd discovered she and Proxima were twins, the Astromancers had decided it was too dangerous for them to be together. Arkayna was forbidden to spend time with her, for fear that the prophecy would come true. Nova Terron had guards watching both of them.

Arkayna and Proxima had managed to sneak away from the Astromancer Academy for just an hour. In that short time, Tazma tracked them across the city and attacked them, putting the whole realm in danger. After that, Nova Terron felt he had no choice but to send Proxima to another realm. Malvaron's aunt, Auntie Yaga, accompanied her to Earth. Now Arkayna was waiting to hear when she could return. How long would it be before they saw each other again? Would Arkayna ever get her sister back?

She sat on the couch, resting her head in her hands.

"Hey, you stressing about Proxima?" Zarya asked, walking over to her.

"You know me so well," Arkayna said. She looked at Zarya gratefully. "We've come a long way, haven't we?"

"A loooong way," Zarya agreed. "A princess and a pauper? BFFs?"

"*You* saying 'BFFs' . . ." That made Arkayna smile.

Zarya wrapped her arm around Arkayna. "Your sister's gonna be fine."

They sat there for a moment, watching Piper and Em play ball with Choko. Then, without any warning, a portal swirled open beside them. Auntie Yaga's van came screeching out of it. All the girls ran behind the couch, ducking for cover.

As the van slowed to a stop, Auntie Yaga stumbled out. She was a large, round woman with curly black hair. She fell into the girls' arms.

"Necrafa captured Proxima . . ." she said.

Arkayna's heart sank. As the other girls helped

Auntie Yaga up and called for Malvaron, Arkayna tried to process what it all meant. Necrafa, the most powerful villain in all of Gemina, had her sister. It was only a matter of time before something terrible happened. Proxima was in grave danger already.

The girls were helping Auntie Yaga onto a stone table as Malvaron rushed in. Em grabbed her hand and held it tight. "Is she going to be okay?" she asked.

"We can only hope," Malvaron said. "This is some seriously dark mojo."

Arkayna stared down at Auntie Yaga, her anger building. Tazma and Necrafa had hurt her and kidnapped Proxima. They had to act.

"Okay, girls," she said, turning to the others. "Let's hit Necrafa's lair and save Proxima."

"Wait!" Malvaron said. "If Necrafa captures you, she'll have *both* twins."

"Right—and she'll be able to raise the Spectral Dragon," Em added.

"And our realm goes kablooey!" Piper cried. "Kapow! Kablammo! Kaboom!"

Everyone turned and stared at Arkayna, waiting for her to speak.

"Maybe you should sit this one out?" Malvaron asked.

"Proxima is my sister," Arkayna said, more certain than ever. "I'm bringing her home."

"We're bringing her home *together.*" Zarya put her hand on Arkayna's shoulder and smiled. Arkayna let out a deep breath, relieved she could count on her friends. Together they headed out to the stables to get their griffins.

TWELVE

THE FOUR MYSTICONS cut through the sky, speeding toward Necrafa's lair. Arkayna led the way, her eyes fixed straight ahead. She was going to get her sister back. No one could stop her, not even Necrafa herself.

"Okay, once we get in, Em, Piper, you search Tazma's lab," Arkayna called out. "Zarya and I will hit the throne room."

"How?" Zarya asked. "Necrafa's lair is going to be swarming with spectres."

"Yeah, we can't just fly in," Piper said.

"Who said anything about flying?" Arkayna asked. "Em, did you bring them?"

Em held up four pink orbs. She tossed them into the sky, and one by one they grew and surrounded each Mysticon, creating an airtight bubble.

The heroes floated off their griffins and splashed down into the ocean around the dark tower. They went deeper and deeper into the murky water, eventually coming up in a hidden cove just below the main entrance. After the Mysticons had left the orbs behind, Arkayna sent Choko up to distract the spectre out front. She needed the element of surprise.

Choko taunted the skeleton for a few minutes, then pounced. While the spectre was yanking Choko off its face, the Mysticons sprung up onto the ledge, aiming their weapons at it.

"Nighty night," Zarya said, and they fired. The skeleton exploded in a cloud of red smoke.

Arkayna and Zarya took off down the tunnel, while Em and Piper went the opposite way, toward the lab. When Arkayna finally got to the throne room, she spotted Proxima, and a lump rose in the back of her throat. Her sister was tied up, her head hanging down as if she'd been knocked unconscious. Four spectres stood guard around her. Arkayna and Zarya hid behind some rocks, trying to figure out how to save her.

Arkayna pointed to the stone column that Proxima was tied to. There were two of them right next to each other. "Those obelisks probably help activate the dragon egg. . . ."

"Not if we have anything to do with it," Zarya whispered, knowing this was their chance. It was only a matter of time before Tazma and Necrafa returned.

The two girls sprung out from their hiding spot. Arkayna blasted a spectre with her Dragon Staff. Zarya leapt into the air and shot at another spectre, destroying it. Arkayna kept firing at the other two until they erupted in a cloud of red smoke.

"Get Proxima," Zarya said. "I'll watch out for Necrafa and Tazma."

Arkayna used her Dragon Staff to propel her up the stone column, right to Proxima. She worked at the magic restraint that tied her sister up. "It's okay, sis," she whispered. "It's me, Arkayna."

"Arkayna?" an evil voice replied. Proxima lifted her head, and in an instant her features changed to Necrafa's skeletal face. She had horrible, beady red eyes and sharp horns. Arkayna tried to get away, but Necrafa ensnared her in a magic web. It had all been a trick—Necrafa had trapped her.

"So the Dragon Mage is the princess," Necrafa said.

"Let go of her!" Zarya cried. She raised her bow to fire, but a dark tendril surrounded her, tying her up. Tazma and General Tibion stood in the doorway to the throne room, holding the real Proxima captive.

"You were right, my queen," Tazma said. "They came to rescue her. Welcome to our humble lair, Princess Arkayna."

Proxima stared up at Arkayna, her eyes wide. "You're a Mysticon?"

"Hey, sis . . ." Arkayna said.

"Finally, the twin stars are here!" Necrafa announced. "Time to unleash the Spectral Dragon!"

She threw Arkayna in the air, slamming her against the stone column. She tied her up with dark magic. Then she threw Proxima onto the other stone pillar and held her there. The dragon's egg floated between them.

Necrafa stood in front of them and raised her hands to the sky, sending a surge of green magic spiraling up the columns. "Arise, my pet! Arise and wreak havoc!" she shouted, letting out an evil laugh.

Arkayna squeezed her eyes shut, but she could feel the energy surrounding her. Every inch of her body was humming with it. Beside her, the egg trembled, about to hatch.

"I'm scared, Arkayna," Proxima said.

"So am I!" Arkayna screamed, feeling the dark energy surge through her. She kept thinking about the prophecy. *Its roars will herald a new dark age, and the realm will be purged by the dragon's rage.*

This was it. This was the beginning of the end.

THIRTEEN

"WHEN THE TWIN stars unite, the spectral beast will take flight!" Necrafa said, repeating lines from the prophecy. She waited for the dragon's egg to hatch, but after a few minutes the magic fizzled out. Proxima and Arkayna just stayed there, tied to the stone pillars, with the egg in between them.

"What . . . what happened?" Necrafa asked, staring down at her hands.

Proxima smiled. "It appears the evil lich hit a glitch."

"Ouch! Dragon buuuurrrrrn," Arkayna said.

"Watch your tongues!" Tazma hissed. Before

Tazma could go on, Necrafa caught her in a web of red magic. The queen's servant was tied up and helpless. "Please . . . I don't know what happened," Tazma said. "The prophecy said—"

"You will come with me," Necrafa ordered Tazma. She flew down the tunnel, dragging Tazma behind her. She turned to General Tibion as she left. "You—guard them."

Arkayna and Proxima watched as Necrafa and Tazma disappeared down the tunnel. More spectres came in to join Tibion. Arkayna struggled to break free of her bonds, but they were too tight. It was starting to feel hopeless.

After a long while, Proxima turned to her. "You were a Mysticon this whole time?"

"I wanted to tell you, I really did," Arkayna said.

"Well, you should have!" Proxima said.

Arkayna wanted to defend herself. They'd barely had any time together before Proxima was kidnapped. When was she supposed to have explained her secret identity? What was she supposed to say? *Yeah, by the way, I'm also the Dragon Mage . . . and that Princess Arkayna you spent the day with while I was at the orphanage? That was actually Choko. Sorry if he peed on anything.*

Suddenly Arkayna realized Proxima was staring at something down the tunnel. Arkayna followed her gaze and saw that Piper and Em were hiding behind some rocks, ready to strike.

Proxima gave Arkayna a look that said, *Play along.* Then she said, "I trusted you, but you didn't feel like you could trust me."

"Give her a break, Proxima," Zarya said from the floor, where she was still tied up. "It ain't easy being a Mysticon."

"Oh, shut it, Mysticon Ranger," Proxima snapped.

"Don't talk to her like that!" Arkayna said.

"And this was your plan?" Proxima continued. "Coming to rescue me, thereby putting the whole realm in jeopardy?"

"Meow, cat fight!" Tibion said. "Settle in, boys, this is going to be good. . . ."

Arkayna couldn't help but smile. "Yes, it is."

"Why are you smiling?" Tibion asked. "The only reason . . . would be if this whole argument was . . . a distraction!"

Just then one of Em's magic orbs hit him in the head, knocking him out. Piper rushed in and threw her Energy Hoops at the other spectres. They went flying into the wall. Em cut Zarya free, and Zarya used her arrows to break the bonds that held Proxima and Arkayna. They both fell to the ground.

Arkayna stood up and tried to steady herself. Even though she was free of Necrafa's magic, she still felt very strange. Energy pulsed through her, and she didn't feel like she could step away from the stone pillar.

"Are you okay?" Em asked.

"I'll be fine . . ." Arkayna said. She turned to

Proxima. Zarya had caught her before she hit the ground. "Nice acting, sis."

"Did I sound believable?" Proxima asked. "I was so nervous."

"You were worried about your acting?" Zarya leaned against the pillar. "You were captured by Necrafa!"

Zarya went to step forward, but she couldn't. The green, swirling energy returned, tying her to the stone column. Arkayna was frozen, too. The energy surged through her and up the pillar. She squeezed her eyes shut, unable to move.

The rest of the Mysticons were blown back by the sudden force of the dragon's egg. Arkayna screamed. She couldn't see or hear anything anymore. The energy was so strong it had completely taken her over.

High above them, the egg trembled. Energy swirled around it. The top of it cracked, and the dragon emerged. The force finally released Zarya and Arkayna. They were thrown forward, off the two pillars, and hit the ground hard.

When Arkayna raised her head, she couldn't believe what she was looking at. Standing in front of them was a two-headed dragon, three times bigger than they were, breathing green fire out of its mouth.

"The Spectral Dragon!" she said, her eyes wide with fear.

FOURTEEN

THE SPECTRE GUARDS struggled to get up and out of the cave. The Mysticons scattered, running in different directions. Em took off and the dragon followed after her. She only had her Star Sword for protection. "Hey! What did we ever do to you?" she called out to the dragon.

That didn't stop it. It charged her, so she put up her shield. She ran away as she blocked each of the dragon's fiery blasts. Then she lured it down a tunnel. She used her shield as a surf-board, skidding around so the dragon's blasts missed her and destroyed a few of the spectres.

After a few minutes, the dragon turned its sights on Piper.

"Snappy little thing, aren't you?" Piper said as she backed up into Zarya.

"I can fix that." Zarya pulled back her bowstring, launching two cable arrows at the dragon's jaws. They wrapped around them, tying the dragon's mouth shut. It gave the Mysticons just enough time to get away. The heroes took off down the tunnel.

"So if we unleashed the Spectral Dragon . . ." Zarya said, turning to Arkayna as she ran, "that means . . ."

"We're the twins . . . ?" Arkayna said.

"No, no, that doesn't make any sense," Proxima said.

"Yeah, maybe we should do the family reunion thing later," Em muttered. The two-headed dragon had broken out of Zarya's bonds and was charging toward them. They'd reached a dead end in the tunnel and were completely trapped.

Em threw up a forcefield just as the dragon blasted them with fire, but the attack was too strong. The forcefield burst. The Mysticons released their avatars, hoping they'd be powerful enough to stop the dragon, but it defeated them with one burst of flame.

Arkayna spun around, searching for a way out. There was a narrow opening in the rocks just a few feet away. It was too small for the dragon to get inside. She didn't know where it went, but it was worth a try. The Mysticons followed her in, and within seconds they were falling through a tunnel. They landed with a thud at the mouth of a cave.

"Quick, to the balcony!" Arkayna said, recognizing where they were. The exit couldn't be far now.

Em ran behind her. "If we can get to the orbs we can—"

"Escape?" Tazma asked, rushing out of another tunnel. Necrafa was right behind her, and her spectres swarmed the air. "Not likely, Mysticons."

Necrafa's head spun around, and dark red magic blasted out of her mouth. The Mysticons fought back with all they had, but it was no use. The queen was too powerful.

"Retreat!" Arkayna ordered, turning back toward the tunnel they had come through.

"Do you remember what's back there?" Piper asked, thinking of the dragon.

Em pulled a magic orb from her pocket. "Here goes nothing!" she said, hurling it toward the opening. It exploded, raining down rocks and dust. But it was no use. The dragon appeared from within the cloud of debris.

"The Spectral Dragon!" Necrafa cried, raising her hands in the air. "The prophecy is fulfilled!"

The Mysticons were surrounded on all sides. Em started to panic. She leaned over, struggling to breathe.

"Someone get the dwarf a paper bag," Zarya said.

"Oh my goblin! My bag!" Piper said, pulling her portal bag off her back.

Necrafa was too focused on the Spectral Dragon to notice what was happening. She floated toward the dragon, her hands outstretched. "Come to me, my beast," she said. "Join with me."

Em opened the bag and stuck her head in, trying to breathe.

"No, don't breathe into it!" Piper said, yanking it back. She put it on the ground. "Jump into it!"

"Your portal bag! Brilliant!" Arkayna said, noticing what was happening.

"Destroy them, my child!" Necrafa ordered.

One by one the Mysticons jumped into the portal bag. The dragon reared back and let loose a horrible torrent of fire, but the girls were already gone. The Mysticons were rocketed through space, the dragon's fire close behind them, and then they all shot out across the floor of the Stronghold's common room. Malvaron and his cyclops friend, Doug, were waiting for them.

"Welcome home," Malvaron said, tossing the portal bag up in the air.

Arkayna destroyed it with her Dragon Staff so no one could follow them through. She was about to explain what happened when Auntie Yaga let out a low moan. She was still on the table where they'd left her.

"Auntie Yaga! You're okay!" Malvaron said. His aunt sat up and rubbed her eyes. While the Mysticons were away, Malvaron had worked with Doug to remove the phantom claw Tazma had driven through her heart.

"To be honest, I've been better," Auntie Yaga said, looking a bit confused. She obviously had trouble with her memory. "I'm never ordering lunch from Earth again. What was that? Heartburn?"

Malvaron, the Mysticons, and Nova Terron
hold the Dragon Disk at the Celestial Forge.

Mysticon Dragon Mage and Proxima face off.

Mysticon Dragon Mage shows Nova Terron
just how angry she is.

Tazma and General Tibion confront the Mysticons.

The Mysticons look through the portal into
Mrs. Sparklebottom's sanctuary.

Em kneels to talk to de-aged, toddler-sized Zarya.

The Mysticons sneak around Mrs. Sparklebottom,
who's distracted by her television.

The Mysticons are caught in Mrs. Sparklebottom's web.

Half-spider Mrs. Sparklebottom confronts Arkayna.

Auntie Yaga steps out of her van at the stronghold
to pass on a desperate message.

Arkayna and Proxima are held captive
with the dragon egg between them.

Necrafa is displeased with Tazma.

The Mysticons discover the truth about Arkayna's sister at the Astromancer Academy.

Necrafa rides the Spectral Dragon toward Drake City.

Arkayna and Zarya navigate spinning energy shields that protect the two golden rings.

Arkayna and Zarya rise into the sky, powered by their twin rings.

Proxima didn't respond. She kept staring at Arkayna and Zarya. "How is this possible?"

"So . . . you two are the twins," Em said.

"You don't look like twins," Piper added.

"According to the prophecy, we are," Arkayna said.

"Well, according to the prophecy . . . we're all doomed," Zarya replied.

"The Spectral Dragon has been released?" Malvaron asked, fear in his voice.

No one had the courage to answer him. Arkayna studied Zarya's face, which she'd looked at a hundred times before. Was this the truth? Was Zarya her real sister? And now that they knew, would they be able to stop Necrafa together?

FIFTEEN

THE MYSTICONS AND Malvaron stood in front of
Nova Terron, Proxima, and Gandobi. They'd
come to the Astromancer Academy for answers.
Auntie Yaga had been saved, and they'd escaped
Necrafa, but Arkayna still had so many questions.
Was the story Nova Terron told them a lie? Had
he known Zarya was her twin all along? Were she
and Proxima related at all?

"This is crazy. How did this even happen?"
Arkayna asked.

"First, Proxima is her sister," Em said, trying
to understand. "But now she's not, because . . ."

"I am?" Zarya finished.

"Perhaps we can discuss this *after* we've dealt with Necrafa?" Gandobi asked.

"We're not saving the realm until we get answers," Arkayna said, pointing her Dragon Staff at Gandobi.

Nova Terron took a deep breath. "Very well. It appears that after I left you in the care of Mrs. Sparklebottom—"

"After you baby-snatched me," Zarya corrected him.

"Yes," Nova Terron agreed. "She took my order to protect your identity seriously, and she switched you. She hid this. Even from me. Proxima's history was a complete fabrication."

At that, Proxima gasped. Without saying a word, she ran out of the Star Chamber, her eyes welling with tears. Arkayna called after her, but she just ignored Arkayna's cry.

"I am truly sorry," Nova Terron continued.

"You tore me from my family," Zarya said, getting right in his face.

"Hey, hey!" Em jumped between them. "The most important thing is you're together again."

She reached down and grabbed Arkayna's and Zarya's hands. Then she put them together. As soon as they touched, Arkayna felt energy surge up her arm. They floated up into the air. An orb of green light glowed between them.

"What's happening?" Arkayna asked. Instinctually, she closed her eyes. When she opened them again, she had a strange vision. She and Zarya were soaring through the night sky. They transformed into their avatars, the Dragon and the Wolf, and then transformed back, stopping right in front of two golden rings. The gold rings were beautiful, but when they reached out to touch them, the rings exploded into nothing more than black smoke. Then Arkayna started falling, her screams echoing in the night.

She hit the ground hard. When she opened her eyes, she realized she was back in the Star Chamber. She and Zarya had fallen out of the air.

"Oh my goblin!" Em screamed. "Are you okay?"

"I think we had a vision . . ." Zarya said, lifting her head.

"Of two rings floating in the air," Arkayna added.

"By the stars," Nova Terron said. "A binary vision."

"Due to your bond as twins," Malvaron explained.

"Morpheum Projectus Animus!" Nova Terron said, raising his hands. One of Gandobi's blank scrolls floated out in front of them. Using his magic, Nova Terron drew the vision from both Arkayna's and Zarya's minds. The visions combined on the black scroll to paint a picture.

"A map," Zarya said, studying it.

"It looks like it leads to Mount Tyrannous," Malvaron said.

"That's where we'll find the rings," Arkayna said.

"What's so special about them?" Piper asked.

"You had a vision of them for a reason," Nova Terron said, holding up his finger. "Fail this quest and you doom the realm."

Arkayna's eyes went wide. She stared at her friends as Nova Terron's words echoed in her ears. *Fail this quest and you doom the realm.*

She'd never been more scared in her life.

ARKAYNA AND ZARYA soared through the air on their griffins. Arkayna knew they didn't have much time. Soon Necrafa would use the Spectral Dragon to attack the city. Arkayna had told Em and Piper to protect Drake City's citizens while she and Zarya went to Mount Tyrannous to retrieve the golden rings from their vision. She hoped they'd be back before it was too late.

"This is awesome!" Zarya called through the rain. She held the map in one hand. "Our first quest."

"We've been on a gazillion quests," Arkayna said.

"Yeah, but this is our first one as sisters," Zarya said.

"Uh-huh . . . look . . . about this sister thing . . ." Arkayna started.

"We're here!" Zarya cried. Straight ahead of them, a beautiful, spiraling tower rose up into the sky. A staircase wrapped around the side of it. Zarya hopped off first and Arkayna jumped into her arms.

"Race you to the top, sis!" Zarya ran up the stairs.

"I miss being an only child," Arkayna muttered under her breath. She ran for what felt like an eternity. The tower went up, higher and higher, and she kept running until her legs hurt. When they finally got to the top, there was a circular platform where they could rest.

"Fifty flights of sheer terror," Arkayna said, trying not to look over the edge.

"I know. Wasn't it awesome?" Zarya asked. "Check it out, the rings!"

Sure enough, the two golden rings were hovering in the middle of the platform. "Quick, let's grab them and go," Arkayna said.

She walked toward them, eager to get the rings as quickly as possible. But before Arkayna could get close, she tripped a series of protection shields. They rose up from the floor and spun around the rings. There were three different spinning layers, each a half-sphere, layered inside one another. They were all a few feet apart.

"Great," Arkayna said. "The vision didn't say anything about razor-sharp protection magic."

"Don't worry, sis." Zarya rubbed Arkayna's head, messing up her tiara. "We got this."

Zarya ran to the other side of the shields and they both stood there for a few minutes, watching the three layers spin. Since each shield was just half a sphere, there were openings between them as they spun around inside one another.

If they got the timing right, they'd be able to cross the shields, one layer at a time.

"Okay, waiting for an opening . . ." Arkayna said. "On three . . . two . . . one . . . go!"

As soon as the first shield spun open, Arkayna and Zarya darted inside. They stood across from each other, sandwiched between the first two spinning layers.

"Nice job, sis! Only two more to go." Zarya smiled. Choko landed next to her and chirped his approval.

"Thanks, but, uh . . . can you ease up on the 'sis' thing?" Arkayna let out an uncomfortable laugh.

"What?" Zarya asked.

"Next opening!" Arkayna said, watching the shields again. "And . . . go!"

They both leapt forward. Now they were right in the center of the spinning shields, just one layer away from the rings.

"You have a problem with me calling you 'sis'?" Zarya asked as soon as she knew she was safe.

"No, it's just . . ." Arkayna struggled to find the right words. How was she supposed to tell Zarya that this was all happening a little too fast? Just yesterday she thought Proxima was her sister. "Go!"

"Wait!" Zarya yelled.

Arkayna jumped first, and Zarya felt she had no choice but to follow. But she was just a second too late moving past the final shield. Its razor-sharp edge nicked her arm. She fell into the center, clutching her elbow in pain.

"Oh my goblin! Let me see your arm," Arkayna said. "I'm so sorry!"

"I'm fine," Zarya snapped.

"Look, this isn't easy, okay?" Arkayna went on. "It's just . . . you and I are so different."

"Forget it," Zarya said. "I never needed family

before, and I don't need it now. Let's just grab these stupid—" She saw it the same time Choko did. "Where did the rings go?"

They turned and saw a cloaked figure at the edge of the circular platform. At some point he must've swooped in and stolen the rings when they weren't looking. Probably when they were fighting.

"After him!" Zarya yelled.

They took off down the stairs, running as fast as they could.

SEVENTEEN

THE CLOAKED FIGURE was always just a little in front of them. Arkayna tried to blast him with magic from her Dragon Staff, but he was moving too fast. She kept missing him.

Just when they were gaining on him, he stopped and spun around. He wielded a giant sword. That's when he let down his hood.

"Dreadbane?" Arkayna said, staring at the giant skeleton warrior. The last time they'd seen him, he was trapped behind Necrafa's portal. She'd banished him to a desert dimension—even after he'd stolen the Codex for her. He was blinded by his love for her, even though she was just using him to destroy the realm.

"In the flesh," he growled through his skeletal jaws. "So to speak . . ."

"He escaped the prison dimension?" Zarya asked as she drew back her bow.

"Give us the rings," Arkayna ordered. "It's the only way to destroy Necrafa."

"Which is why she must have them," Dreadbane said.

"She tried to abandon you," Zarya shot back.

"Our love is . . . *complicated*." With that, he hurled his sword at them. It landed on the stairs just below them and exploded, destroying a huge chunk of stone. The force of the blast threw Arkayna backward, and in an instant she was plummeting off the tower.

"Long live Necrafa!" Dreadbane yelled as he ran away.

"Hang on!" Zarya shouted as she shot a magic arrow at Arkayna. She was able to grab the rope trailing it and swing onto the side of the tower. But she was still thirty feet below Zarya and Choko. They pulled her up inch by inch until she was back on the stairs.

Arkayna struggled to catch her breath. When she was certain she was safe, she turned to Zarya. Zarya had always been one of the bravest and strongest people she knew. She never hesitated in the face of danger. And she would do anything for the people she loved.

"Thanks . . . sis," Arkayna said.

"Don't mention it," Zarya said, turning to go.

"Wait . . . I'm sorry I didn't seem happy that you are my sister," Arkayna said. "It's just . . . with the prophecy and Proxima and everything else, it's been so confusing. But I'm happy. I am."

Zarya still seemed unsure. Her shoulders were slumped and she wouldn't look at Arkayna.

"No, for real. I love you," Arkayna said. She punched Zarya in the arm, then gave her a noogie. "I love you, I love you!"

"Okay!" Zarya finally said. She was smiling. "That's more like it."

But Arkayna wasn't done. She wrapped her arms around Zarya, enjoying how good it felt to be close to her. "I love you, sis."

"Right. The 'sis' thing *is* kinda annoying," Zarya laughed. "Now let's get that bone dome and save the realm."

They took off on their griffins, swooping down across the city. It was clear Necrafa had already been there. Bridges were destroyed and buildings had collapsed. There were giant patches of black, scorched earth. As they got closer they could see the other Mysticons on top of a roof. They were with the Sky Pirate captain named Kitty, her trusted lieutenant (and little brother) Kasey, and the rest of her crew. It was clear Em and Piper had called them in for help.

Necrafa was hovering in the air high above them. She rode the Spectral Dragon and had a whole army of spectres behind her.

Arkayna's stomach sank. She was more power-ful than all of them combined, and they hadn't returned with the rings. How much longer could they hold off her army? Were they already doomed?

"They're back!" Piper yelled when she spotted them. She turned to Necrafa. "You're in trouble now! Hit her with the rings, girls!"

Arkayna and Zarya jumped down onto the roof. "We don't have them," Arkayna confessed.

"If you don't have the rings, who does?" Em asked.

Dreadbane swooped down right on cue. He was riding his vulture. He held the glowing rings up in his hand.

"I do!" he yelled. "They belong to my queen!"

EIGHTEEN

"VERY GOOD," NECRAFA said as she gazed down at Dreadbane. She waved him toward her. "Bring me the rings."

Arkayna knew this was it. If she didn't get the rings back now, the whole realm would be destroyed. She jumped back onto her griffin and flew up in the air to talk to Dreadbane. "Don't," she pleaded. "She doesn't love you, Dreadbane."

"Lies!" Necrafa snapped. "Together we will purge the realm with the dragon's rage."

"You have to fight for the things you love," Arkayna urged. "Your home. Your friends. Your starmates. Your sisters. But there's nothing you can do to make them love you back."

"Tell me you love me," Dreadbane said, looking up at Necrafa.

"I love you," she lied.

"Don't listen to her, Dreadbane!" Arkayna begged.

"I love you, I love you, I love you!" Necrafa grew angrier each time she said it. Dreadbane stared up at her, his eyes sad, like he wasn't sure what to do. "Now, give me the rings!"

Dreadbane clutched the rings in his hand. He didn't move. He looked up at Necrafa, then back at Arkayna. He seemed confused.

Necrafa couldn't take it any longer. She blasted him with her dark magic, letting him wither in pain.

"I hate you, you worthless pile of bones!" she snapped. "Give me the rings!"

She blasted Dreadbane again. When he sat back up, he had tears in his eyes. "Alas,

Necrafa . . ." He held the rings away from him. "It's time for me to let go."

He released the rings and they fell toward the ground. Necrafa grabbed them with her magic, drawing them up toward her in the sky.

But Zarya acted fast. She aimed up and shot an arrow at Necrafa. It sailed past the rings and high into the air.

"Ha! You missed!" Necrafa laughed.

"I never miss," Zarya said. As the arrow came back down, it took the two rings from Necrafa and brought them down to the roof. Arkayna and Zarya raised their hands up and a golden ring slipped onto each girl's finger.

"The prophecy was right," Arkayna said. "The realm will be purged by the dragon's rage."

"But not your dragon," Zarya said.

"Ours," Arkayna and Zarya said together. "Unleash the twin dragons!"

Powered by the energy of their rings, Arkayna and Zarya shot into the night sky in a swirl of energy. Together they transformed into two fierce Dragon avatars. They spun around each other, soaring up toward the moon, and let out a fearsome roar.

Then they set their sights on Necrafa. She charged toward them on the Spectral Dragon and they zoomed down to meet her. They collided in a huge explosion of light and sound.

"No!" Necrafa screamed. "Noooo! Noooo!"

Arkayna couldn't see a thing. The light was blinding. Her and Zarya's powers had never been stronger, and the energy surged through them, creating a glowing green orb. Then the energy around them exploded, sending a ripple of magic through the city. In seconds, Necrafa and all of her spectres were gone.

NINETEEN

"BY THE HAMMER of Harmon!" Em yelled as Arkayna and Zarya dove to the ground, now transformed back into their Mysticon identities. They landed on the roof. Arkayna's hands were still trembling.

"That was fab-tacular!" Piper cried.

"Did we get her?" Zarya asked, looking around.

"Did we destroy Necrafa?" Arkayna couldn't believe it was true.

"Did we ever!" a familiar voice called out. The Mysticons turned to see Gawayne, Arkayna's stepbrother, who ruled the city now that their parents were trapped in bone. He was hanging out of the top of a limo, his butler right beside him. Hundreds of grateful citizens surrounded him.

"Get in here, girls," he called out to them. "Come on, hug it out. Butler, prepare a victory party—no, wait—a victory *fiesta* for the entire city."

He leapt out of the limo at the Mysticons, then threw his arms around them in a hug. Arkayna closed her eyes, already annoyed with her stepbrother. He hadn't done a thing and he was trying to take all the credit, as usual.

"We make a great team," Gawayne sighed.

That night, the sky exploded with fireworks. The balcony of the Royal Tower was packed with people. The Sky Pirates danced and sang to the music, and even Choko busted a move. Arkayna hated to admit it, but Gawayne had thrown an incredible party. He could at least do one thing right.

"Oh my goblin, this is going to be amazing," Arkayna said to Zarya as they considered their new sisterhood. They were sitting beside each other on a couch, hanging out with Kitty and Malvaron. Arkayna kept thinking about how cool it was that they were in the Royal Tower together, the same place their mother had lived for so many years. There were so many things she and Zarya still had to do and say to each other. "We can stay up all night and tell each other secrets! We can start sister diaries together! Oh, I have to get you your own quill!"

"Quills . . . I love quills . . ." Zarya said skeptically.

"You wanted her to be happy," Kitty said to Zarya as Malvaron invited Arkayna to dance. "She's happy."

Arkayna pretended she hadn't heard them as she twirled around the dance floor with Malvaron. It never felt so right to be back in the Royal Tower, where she grew up, with the twin sister she never knew she had. As confusing as the past few days had been, she was grateful for everything that had happened. And most of all, she was grateful that she didn't have to worry about the prophecy coming true.

Arkayna spotted Proxima at the far end of the roof. She'd looked so hurt when the truth came out, and everything had happened so fast Arkayna hadn't gotten a chance to talk to her yet. The secrets Nova Terron kept had been devastating for all of them, but finding out you aren't who you think you are? Arkayna would have to find time to make sure Proxima was all right.

But for now, Arkayna was determined to enjoy the moment. She spun around once, then again, letting the music cheer her. She looked up into Malvaron's sweet brown eyes, and for the first time in a long time she felt safe and happy. The realm of Gemina was finally at peace. She wanted this feeling to last forever.

Was that too much to ask?

DISCOVER ANOTHER NOVELIZATION AND ALL-NEW MYSTICONS ADVENTURES!

AVAILABLE NOW WHEREVER BOOKS ARE SOLD!